FAMILIAR SPIRITS

EMERE

OLATINWO ADEAGBO FATOKI

DEDICATION

I dedicate this book to the Almighty God, my country and my state, the city of Ibadan and Kúṣeélá Village as well as residents of Igbó Elérin and environs in Lagelu Local Government Area. I have a passion for the development of the area and will do all within my power to work for its advancement.

This book is also dedicated to parents who have experienced the misfortune of having familiar spirit children, all women in the Fatoki family, my friends, my teachers from the primary school to the tertiary level aswell as my co-workers over the years.

Also, I dedicate this book to the late Oba Yesufu Oloyede Asanike, His royal Majesty the Olubadan of Ibadan land during whose reign the first ever Ibadan indigene, Dr. Omololu Olunloyo assumed the exalted office of the Executive Governor of Oyo State.

Finally, this book is dedicated to late Chief Bola Ige, an Esa-Oke indigene and first Executive Governor of old Oyo State who was married to an Ibadan indigene, late Atinuke Oloko. He introduced free secondary education in the state. He was widely acclaimed for his selflessness and commitment to the cause of the downtrodden.

PREFACE

The inspiration to write this book came from the beliefs of people about their attitudes to the children known as familiar spirits.

Many regard these children as those born-to-die and return in a cycle of going and coming, members of evil societies, Ogbanje, mysterious children, children that disappear and return with air, demonic children and elements. These tags underscore the difficulties associated with true identity of familiar spirits. To clarify these misconceptions, I, pondered over the issues and came to the facts that children spirits are products of reincarnation and are awe-inspiring characters. They are power personified. The (invisible) spirits working with them are equally enigmatic. Familiar spirits are indeed like a mystery wrapped in an enigma. They are capricious, and capable of bringing misfortune to their parents.

On the question of power, they are of a higher order than witches and wizards. My mothers who kill without brandishing a sword, homage! Familiar spirits can enter the womb of pregnant women with ease. Who is there to query them? A familiar spirit possesses the power to transform into a baby, expel the one inside a pregnant woman's womb and replace him/her.

They have the power to impoverish their parents; inflict sufferings and they may choose to assume dual personality status: they can move about while yet unborn.

They hold regular nocturnal meetings. Venues include the air, inside the water, in the bush, at crossroads and beside walls like lizards. They face wall while asleep.

At meetings they eat sand, (which is symbolic of rice) and banana. The claim that they drink blood or greenwater could not be authenticated. They deliberate on knotty issues in their meetings, which include whether to impoverish or enrich their parents, how to uplift or downgrade a person, project, town, state, country and or the world at large. They are marksmen: they shoot without missing their target. They rarely give up, in the pursuit of their goals. By their nature and character, they are disrespectful, and hardly ever make distinctions between their peers and elders. Like serpents, they lack the milk of mercy. They don't assist people financially, and can plunge people into life-long anguish. To be candid, majority of them are the quintessence of beauty while some are ugly and as dirty as pigs. In the long run, no familiar spirit ever goes scot free, while some are dullards by choice in order to fritter away the parents financial resources and cause them tears, some may choose to be exceptionally brilliant and wise like Agboniregun but die in their prime, thereby throwing their parents into deep mourning.

To make a familiar spirit live long either by traditional religious means or other methods, the familiar spirit must as a first step, confess his or her status as well as his/her involvement with the group. Without this, no prayer or charm can avail. It's after a familiar spirit has confessed that a seasoned prophet can fast and pray for prolongation of his or her life.

In the traditional way, after a familiar spirit has confessed to a Babalawo or Juju man who knows his onions that he/she is a familiar spirit, the medicine man would recommend that certain terms be packed as a gift to the familiar spirit group. The package is made up of the following items:

(a) A white calabash in which the articles will be packed

(b) White cloth

(c) Palm oil

(d) A black goat

(e) One hundred and forty cowries shells

(f) Ekuru

(g) Beans

(h) A black coffin

(i) Nine pieces of abata kolanuts

(g) Nine bitter kola (this will cleanse the group member of bitterness)

(K) A plantain trunk

Now, let's undertake a trip to the camp of the initiated, the forest of the callous-familiar-spirit groups in order to gain insight into the lifestyles of these mysterious beings.

Ọlátińwọ́ Adéagbo Fátókí

Ibàdan, Nigeria

January 2020

ACKNOWLEDGEMENTS

I wish to express my sincere appreciation to Late pa Samuel Omotosho Adediran, a retired police boss, the Toso of Dalegan of Ajia in Egbeda Local Government Area of Oyo State who was also the first Mogaji of Agbo Compound of Ojaigbo in Ibadan who gave his daughter, Detola to me as wife, relationship I have never nor will ever regret.

I acknowledge my mother in-law, the Isan-Ekiti born late Mama Felicia Funmilayo Fayemi. I also appreciate my nephews and nieces (the grandchildren of my dad, the late Adeagbo Fatoki) who have been tremendous blessing to me.

Prof. Oloruntoyin Omoyeni Falola and Messrs Gbenga Ibikunle, Bioye Oloyede, late Gboyega Ola-Balogun and Dr Olabisi Kayode Ayedun (Biskay), all of whom are friends in need. Olawuwo Benjamin Olutoki and Olusegun Adeagbo Fatoki, both of whom have lend credence to the saying that blood is thicker than water.

Finally, I appreciate all my friends either from within my maternal or paternal family, or outside of families all whom have contributed greatly to making me what I am today.

CAST

Leader
Fiery eye
Little devil
Rich man's terror
Mammy water
Olóríẹgbẹ́
Ojúufáñtà
Hunter (Odegbàmií)
Rich man
Alàke
Segi
Crowd
Old woman
Oderindé and other hunters
Congregation
Pastor
Sunmónu
Bolá
Túndùn
Àlàdé
Fúnmi
Awógbàmí
Kékeréawo
Hunters

ACT 1 SCENE 1

(In the heavenlies a gathering of familiar spirits seated as chairman is their leader. He invites his members to the podium one after the other, to tell everybody their names and nationalities. His crown is made of an admixture of gold and bronze. He is enthroned as king. The attire of each of the familiar spirits is awe-inspiring, the sight of which will make humans take to their heels.)

Leader:

    Heeeheeee!

    Heeeheeee!

(His voice rises in tempo with each shout)

    My children-en-en

    Where have you been?

    It is I, Mole, your leader

    That is calling you

    Can the lion roar

    And other animals not tremble?

    Was it ever heard that a child declines to answer his mother's call?

    A nursing mother cannot turn deaf ears to the anguished cry of her child.

    I am calling you

    Answer me now

    My children-en-en

(Responses are heard from every road that leads to the to the meeting place. The voices are esoteric and guttural, like masquerades: Benbe

drums beat somberly underneath.)

Voices: Ye-e-e-s!

> We are here, father
>
> Is there any mountain that is higher than heaven?
>
> You are our father
>
> You are greater than our great fathers
>
> You're the mountain that is highly exalted
>
> Above all other mountains
>
> Homage!
>
> We are responding
>
> When a nursing mother hears the anguished cry of her infant
>
> She cannot but respond
>
> We are here, father

(They start coming in one after the other, their steppings and dancing rhythmically rhyming with the low Benbe drumming. In a melodious voice).

> We are here
>
> We fearful ones, terror to pregnant women, we that shun morning outings and refuse to go out in the evening ether, our favourite leisure-hour is one o'clock. Whenever we embark on nocturnal outing any pregnant woman that roams the street at midday will get what she's so desperately looking for!
>
> You loiter about in the dark
>
> Once we wink at your baby
>
> The baby vanishes instantly
>
> We will enter your womb
>
> And have a jolly good time
>
> We are here

Our king

Head of familiar spirits worldwide

Fearsome masquerade

Terrifying serpent

Diligent leader

The uncompromising one

The one whose orders are irreversible

We are yours

On our knees we grovel before you

We have no other father beside you

You're the one and only

Head of familiar spirits universal

(As they file in, they pay homage to their leader. After they are all seated, their leader brings out a register, and starts calling their names one after the other, and each of them responds accordingly. Each of them then mounts the podium and speaks boastfully about the power he/she possesses. Next they are allotted to various homes given the dates they are to die).

Leader:

Yuuyuu, Come forward *(with a wry smile)* this is a new face, who brought you here?

Fiery Eye:

I reverence you, long may you live for us, My name is Fiery Eye. I was brought to this meeting for a special purpose by Rich man's terror. As you are aware that we all have places where we constitute a thorn in people's flesh and it is when we want to embark on important journeys that we attend this meeting.

Leader:

Little Devil, go through the financial records. Is he up to date in his obligations?

Little Devil: *(Examines the records)* My lord, the terrible fear that grips-mankind, the invincible one, he has paid his dues, but the treasurer, free spender that he is, has just informed me that he has spent two thousand out of it.

Leader:

(He enters into spiritual possess, mammy water pours water on his head).

Huuhuu

Wahuwahu

Wadopado

He that eats the obligation with the anus water

Palm oil

Remedy

Hin-in-hin!

Are you ready to pay the money?

Treasurer:

Yes, I am. I am ready to pay the money.

Leader: Collect the money from him.

Time is not on our side.

(Fiery Eye kneels before the leader after the treasurer has paid).

Fiery Eye: My Lord.

I, Fiery Eye, want to undertake a trip to the world. I need your permission to be born into the family of a man called Team Leader *(Olóríẹgbẹ́)* at Kotonfe village. I want his fair-complexioned wife to be my mother. You will recall that in ancient times, he and I were born in that village. I am sure he can't recognize me any longer, but he was my benefactor. Presently he is childless. He will be overjoyed if I go as a male child.

Leader: *(Brings out a pot containing green water)*

Tell me, what do you seek in addition, before I dip my rod into water in confirmation of your request?

Fiery Eye: Long may you live, baba.

Once my mother is delivered of me and the family raises a fire inside the room to generate heat for their new born baby, immediately the first firewood they put inside the tripod burns out I want to appear in your presence, the head of familiar spirits worldwide. As we are rejoicing, a cry of anguish shall be raised in Olóríẹgbẹ́'s house (all the other familiar sprits clap, and laugh. They dance for some time before the leader speaks).

Leader: Fiery Eye, this is your name here from today.

Kneel down for me to pray for you.

(Fiery Eye kneels, and the leader begins to chant incantations in an esoteric tone, while others shout, "may it be so").

Power from the north

Run quickly, send power to me

Power from the East

Run quickly send power to me

Power from the west join forces with the South

Run quickly here

The dog runs speedily to its owner

When a goat dips its mouth into salt

It finishes it

Run quickly to me

Power from the four corners of the earth, gather to me

Heavenly power, come speedily

Come quickly to me

Because whatever concerns Fiery Eye

Must be treated with urgency

It is forbidden for Baba

To see clearly

I need your mandate

Empower Fiery Eye

To walk without stumbling

Let him achieve his goal

The wind cannot uproot stubborn grass

The whirlwind cannot carry thick ogi

Fiery Eye's secret must not be exposed

To the world

Let his desires be fulfilled

Leader: (He again enters into a possess Mammy-Water, pours water on his head)

Wahu-wahu-wasi-wasa

Wasala-wasala-wasanke

Water, palm oil, water, palm oil, water!

Remedy!

Remedy!

Remedy!

Come down

(His eyes become clear. Benbe drumming increases tempo, the leader dances, shortly, he directs Little Devil to invite the next person to choose a destiny)

Leader: Little Devil, who's the next person?

Little Devil: Rich Man's Terror

Leader: Where's he?

Rich Man's Terror: Here I am, my Lord

(Starts singing)

The fearful one that terrifies humans

My lord that snatches others' wives to add to his barren

Terror that walks in thick darkness

Head of all enigmatic creatures

Afternoon terror that terrifies pregnant woman

I pay homage to you!

Leader: He ee e e

Has your group paid its dues?

Rich Man's Terror:

I am not in a position to answer for the group but I have paid mine.

Leader: What's that supposed to mean?

I want to know if your group has paid its dues. Never again should you be flippant with me, otherwise the earth will swallow you up.

Rich Man's Terror: I am not on the finance committee

Therefore, I can't say whether our group has paid its dues or not. It's not as if I wanted to slow down the pace of progress.

Leader: Do you know where you are?

I have observed your tendency towards garrulousness each time you're here, and your boastfulness, I'm going to punish you severely. While I won't want anybody to accuse me of high-handedness, I have to warn you that unless I see a change, you're going to pay dearly for your arrogance.

Members: *(Yell at Rich Mans Terror)*

Prostrate! Leader, don't be annoyed, Rich Man's Terror, be careful. Whoever God has appointed as leader deserves honour, irrespective of age. Honour the head, respect the leader. This is Our head and we won't allow anybody to dishonour him.

Rich Man's Terror: *(refuses to honour the leader, neither would he ask for forgiveness)*

Why are you all shouting on me? What is that strange

thing I have done? Although I know that leaders must be respected, this society is for everybody and I won't subscribe to the idea of an individual turning himself into a bully.

(A member signals to him to keepquiet, and he changes gear).

Well, in view of the supremacy of the group and the authority conferred on the leader, I, Rich Man's Terror hereby plead for forgiveness for any embarrassment my conduct and personal composure might have caused the leader and the generality of members of this society.

Members: Alright. Forgive him

Leader: Your plea is accepted.

Rich Man's Terror tell us your desires, and all shall be granted.

Rich Man's Terror: I crave your indulgence to be born

into a rich man's family. I want to be his favourite an exceptionally brilliant child but a sickly one. I want my father to be expending one third of his earnings on my sickness. After my father must have become a financial wreck, I would want him to send one of his drivers to take me and my five younger siblings to a prayer meeting at a church to which the car shall get involved in a lone accident and we shall all perish. I want the driver to be one of our members. I want this crisis to hit my parents in their old age, when it will be impossible for them to bear children.

Leader: *(Everybody shouts for joy)*

I had thought you were going to ask for precious things. Because you have chosen to traumatize your parents on behalf of this society, I hereby grant your request. You may go.

(He looks up, and tells his members to hasten up deeply time is far spent.)

Leader: Little devil, I want everything to be done quickly.

We have to work hard, and time is not on our side. Call the next person. My mother will soon wake up in the world and I want to go back quickly before she does.

Little Devil: Mammy water!

Mammy Water: Present

Little Devil: Come forward

(*Mammy Water, a very beautiful woman comes out, walking majestically like a queen*).

Leader: Walk fast, our mother.

Why don't you dwell in the air, and from there be our matron). Do you think there is pleasure for you in the World? Think deeply.

Mammy Water: Leader, I greet you

I am a familiar spirit that is more powerful than thousands of witches.

I, the invincible that puts the Medicine man to shame.

I turn the medicine man to a liar.

I turn the expert to a novice

I find fulfillment in bringing grief upon my father

I bring sickness upon people to avenge my mother

I that no human being can tame

From the outside, I know the type of child that a pregnant woman is carrying

I am awe-inspiring girl that sends a baby

Packing from its mother's womb

So as to make way for myself

I turn children into handicapped ones

I kill those I chose

What of pregnant women I have killed during labour?

Who can count their number?

Let the person tell us!

I, mammy water that turn the wealthy individual to a pauper.

I am a familiar spirit

The storms of life cannot carry me.

Familiar Spirit!

(She burst into a song and starts dancing, the other familiar spirits dance with her, but the leader remains seated as they dance forward and backward.)

I have come, I have come

Pretty lady

I have come, I have come

Pretty lady

I have come, I have come

Pretty lady

(Drumming ceases. Mammy Water kneels)

I am ready to traverse the earth again.

With your permission, I am ready to go.

Upon my return from the trip, that

I shall become the matron of this society.

I desire to leave

Leader: Mammy Water, our matron.

The one that uses silver to appease a weeping child merciful mother...

(Faces other members)

Rise up, and welcome our mother Mother

All: Mother of the whole wide world familiar spirits

Fights for her peers

Terror of the medicine man

Mother

Leader: Little Devil,

For formality sake, check the financial records for me. Is her Group up-to-date as regards the payment of their annual dues?

Little Devil: Don't you trust them.

Our mother is the society's chairperson. She won't have been here without having fulfilled all her financial obligations

Leader: Mother, what are your requests?

They shall all be granted.

Mammy Water: My Lord, I desire to be born into an average family. I want a textile dealer for a mother, and an itinerant trader for a father.

I want to have formal education, but I don'twant to be a prodigy, I want to help my parents to uplift their business whenever it's about to crumble. I want to be a lone child. At the age of eighteen, I want to graduate from secondary school and die the same day, and I want my parents to remain barren for the rest of their lives. I want my death to cause them a life-long anguish.

Leader: I reluctantly release you.

You will enjoy the world but have it at the back of your mind that all your children are awaiting your return. We can visit you anytime, Always remember to give us money and food.

(Faces the members)

In the absence of any other matter for discussion, I demand that somebody should move a motion for adjournment of the meeting.

Rich Man's Terror: I move the motion for an

adjournment of this meeting.

Fiery Eye: Seconded

Leader: Mammy Water,

Pray for us, after the prayer Little Devil should lead us in choruses.

Mammy Water:

(*As she speaks, others shout*)

> Hee! (in unison)
>
> Awarawuru we-Heee!
>
> Yuuyuu - HEE
>
> Awarawuruwa - Hee!
>
> Long live familiar spirits - Ese
>
> We leaders of born-to-die children
>
> Shall enjoy longevity - Ese
>
> The Rulers of the light shall live long - Ese
>
> We shall live forever - E se
>
> We shall not die - E se
>
> Unchangeable decree
>
> Is that of sugar cane -Ese
>
> May it be so -Ese

Leader: Little Devil, lead us in songs.

> As we sing let us disperse to the four corners of the earth.

Little Devil: (*They sing the song melodiously thrice*)

> We are moving about
>
> To enter into pregnant women
>
> That go to the river side
>
> To turn the wealthy into paupers
>
> To turn the poor into wealthy people
>
> If our mothers die at childbirth, it is of no concern to us
>
> We are not moved by anybody's death
>
> We are not bothered by anybody's demise
>
> We turn slaves to sons
>
> And sons to slaves
>
> Whoever becomes a pauper is not our concern

Any king that fails to reckon with us
Is bound to lose his crown
Any chief that despises us will be
Disgraced out of office
We are traversing the earth- Ese
(Light fades as they disperse).

ACT 1, SCENE 2

(Under a big tree at about one O' clock in the afternoon, low sounds of gong goje, bata and gbedu drumming are heard. Rich Man's Terror, Fiery eye and Mammy Water are dancing; they are dressed in white and white cap and headgear and wear white bangles on their wrists).

Fiery Eye: *(jumps down from the tree and dances like a hunter)*

Today is D-day

I want to make history

I want to teach the human race

Far reaching lessons

I shall become known

To those ignoramuses

Whether the world like it

Or the heaven falls

I must enter a pregnant woman today

I must chase away the child in her womb

I will pluck out its eyes

I will stab the baby's tummy with knife

And take its place

(dances a little, and sits. Mammy Water enters and begins to chant Rara)

Mammy Water: *(dances like a bride)*

I hold on to money

I prefer money to every other thing

I want to meet with wealth at home

So that the whole world may love me

So that mother may dote on me

So that father may hold me in high esteem

I want to be a precious lone child

So that everybody may venerate me

When I am fully grown

With ripe breasts

I SHALL DIE

So that mother will be childless

Father will be childless

And everybody will pity the fate

Of my parents

(She sits beside Fiery Eye, Rich Man's Terrors comes upstage like a warrior and starts singing).

Rich Man's Terror:

We have come to fight the battles of life

It is the brave that can face wars

I am brave and can face wars

I am related to rich people

I have no association with the poor

If a rich person becomes a slave

How does it concern me?

If a socialite becomes a slave

And an acclaimed personality

Goes into oblivion

A rich man begins to suffer

Once the war is won

What concerns me?

If I undertake a journey

And I come across a rich man

I look at the rich man with anger

In my heart

I charge at rich men

In order to render them poor

So they can become handkerchiefs

For people to blow mucus

I have come to the world independently

And I'm engaged in my favourite trade

It is the mighty that fight wars

I, the terror that shakes the rich man mightily

(The drumming rises in tempo)

Today is going to be tough

Let each parent warn their children

Today is going to be tough

My peers, today is going to be tough

Let the husband warn his wife

Today is going to be tough

(He dances and smiles drily. The leader enters just as Rich Man's Terror sits. They all bow to the leader, and he waves at them).

All: We prostrate before you

We kneel down before you our father

The terrible one and father of the world's

Familiar Spirits.

The unconquerable one

One before whom charms are useless

Witches die while trying to hurt you

Wizards try but give up in defeat

A historical being, a phenomena really!

The world's juju men team up - Hin-in

In a bid to bind my father - Hin-in

They tie black and white strings together - Hin-in

They head for the crossroads - Hin-in

Unaware that my father is watching them - Hin-in

As they want to render the final sacrifice Hin-in

My father appears to them Hin-in

He brings fear upon them Hin-in

Should they go forward? Hin-in o

Should they go backward? Hin-in

Long they search for a way - Hin-in

But find none - Hin-in

Fire erupts all of a sudden - Hin-in

Their charms are consumed by the

Conflagration Hin-in

Baba order them to leave

So they could have a story to tell on earth Hin-in

A story to tell over and over - Hin-in

(The drumming change to woro)

Father, welcome

High methodical one

Welcome father

Good father

Welcome!

(After the praise-singing, they start their meeting under a tree, unaware that a hunter is ensconced, hearing them and seeing them clearly).

Leader: Welcome, that WAS A GOOD display.

Familiar spirits shall never be eliminated. My mother had almost woken up before I reached home after our last meeting in the air. Therefore, I enjoin you all to make our deliberations brief today. Fiery Eye, in line with your request to be born into Olóríẹgbẹ́'s household, we shall leave you here. His wife cannot but come to this farm every day.

Any woman that you see here, enter her womb, she's the one.

These two (points at them) will go with me, that I can arrange for them also. Always remember that you are returning immediately the first firewood they use to heat the houseburns out.

(He stands transfixed, looking upwards)

Familiar Spirits in the skies

Invisible familiar spirits

May it be so

(He holds the other two by the hands, and they wave to Fiery Eyes as they leave).

A leaf must keep faith with its appointment with the earth

Olóríẹgbẹ́'s wife must come to the farm today

She should tread the path

And encounter Familiar Spirits in action o

Her coming to the farm is a must!

ART 1, SCENE 3

(At Olóríẹgbẹ́'s house. His wife Ojúufántà wakes and kneels before Olóríẹgbẹ́).

Ojuufanta: *(Kneels before Oloriegbe)*

> My husband, good morning, Ajàní, who has his roots in tree. Good morning.

Olóríẹgbẹ́: *(sits outside brushing his teeth with a chewing stick)*

> Ojúufántà, Asake Iji, their daughter at Ilofa, good morning. You have woken up early this morning. I hope all is well. I'm scared.

Ojúufántà: Don't be scared, I only want to dash to the

> farm, I need some pepper and vegetable for lunch. You know that a pregnant woman should not walk in the noonday.

Olóríẹgbẹ́: That's alright. Go quickly

> *(Shortly after Ojúufántà's' exit through the back door, the hunter enters through the front door, he meets Olóríẹgbẹ́ where he's seated outside).*

Hunter: Greeting to the occupants of this house, a goat

> that refuses to greet gets tied to the stake. A sheep that refuses to greet gets tied tightly to the stake.
>
> I am different from goat and sheep
>
> That's why I greet ahead of my entry.

Olóríẹgbẹ́: Hunter, I hope nothing is amiss. You'vecome

> so early

Hunter: There is no problem. All is well

Olóríẹgbẹ́: Where's the meat you've brought for me?

Hunter: Meat? I killed only a small rodent and that's what
my wife and I use to eat àmàlà in the afternoon.
What of Ojúufántà?

Olóríęgbę: She's just left for the farm.
In fact you almost met her.

Hunter: Oh! Why did you allow her to go?

Olóríęgbę: I hope there is no problem. What is the matter? Come out with it.

Hunter: There isn't much problem, but whatever I tell
you should be treated in strict confidence. It is not for
third party consumption

(pauses, and then talks in a low voice).

Silence is golden. Is it not better for me to keep the secret
to myself? Some lost their life for divulging a secret.

Olóríęgbę: Hunter, what's the matter?
Don't keep me in the dark. No matter how weighty a matter is, it has to be discussed. The worst is for you to report
that you've caught Ojúufántà red-handed in immorality.
Don't keep me in suspense.

Hunter: Immorality?

Can a pregnant woman be involved in infidelity? I have
come to report what I saw during my hunting expedition.
Olóríęgbę, I saw the familiar spirits at their meeting. They
were four and the meeting was...

Olóríęgbę: Hunter, can you recognize familiar spirit?
Show one to me.

Hunter: You can't see them with your naked eyes.
You think it's that simple. That's why I'm greater than you.
I was six years old when my father washed my eyes with
leaf to make me see into the spirit realm. That's the power
of the Osanyin. There's nothing that I cannot see.

Olóríęgbę: You're so boastful, Well, go on with story.

Hunter: Yes! Familiar Spirits.

Olóríẹgbẹ́: I have things to attend to.

If you don't want to talk you can go.

Hunter: Olóríẹgbẹ́, as they were holding their meeting,

I heard one of them say he wanted to bring calamity upon your wife. He revealed that both of them originated from Kotonka and that she was his benefactor. The most astonishing aspect is his statement that he is going to die immediately the first firewood you use to generate heat for him burns out.

Olóríẹgbẹ́: Hunter, are you sure?

Why did I allow the woman to go to the farm? This is incredible!

Hunter: Maybe if I had arrived earlier,

she wouldn't have gone. What shall we do?

Their leader promised to exert all his influence on your wife to get her to the farm today.

Olóríẹgbẹ́: You don't mean it!

Where did you see them?

Hunter: I saw them under the Irókò tree along the path to Koteye-emin brook.

Olóríẹgbẹ́: *(crying)* What shall I do now?

Hunter: All hope is not lost.

It is you our elders who say that when a child has mastered the art of dying in the dry season, the parents would learn to bury him by the riverside. Since they have spoken about firewood, their power is broken. Once the child is born, use a pile of banana trunks to generate heat for him, and the problem is solved!

Olóríẹgbẹ́: Thank you. May God bail us out

(On the farm, Ojúufáńtà suspects that something enters her womb).

Ojúufáńtà: What kind of sign is this?

I have to head for home.

(Back home, Ojúufáńtà meets her husband and the hunter).

Ojúufáńtà: Hunter, good morning. I hope all is well.

Hunter: Thank you, there is no problem.

(Ojúufáńtà goes inside)

Hunter: Olóríẹgbẹ́, it has happened, I'm going,

but don't forget our pact.

Olóríẹgbẹ́: How can I thank you?

I pray that she delivers safely.

(The hunter rises, while Olóríẹgbẹ́ goes in

Ojúufáńtà: My husband,

I hope you are not angry that I lingered a little.

Olóríẹgbẹ́: You didn't linger.

How was the farm? Did you get the pepper?

Ojúufáńtà: I got it but something ominous happened.

As I reached the iroko tree and was about to start removing the pepper from the trees, my head suddenly became swollen and it appeared as if something forcefully entered into my womb. Till now I can't get over the shock.

Olóríẹgbẹ́: There is no problem.

Such happens to pregnant women.

Ojúufáńtà:

What brought the hunter so early in the morning?

Olóríẹgbẹ́: It was a village matter.

Ojúufáńtà: Let me go and cook quickly.

(She goes to the backyard. Olóríẹgbẹ́ also rises, soliloquizing. Simultaneously at a road junction, stand leader of the familiar spirits, Mammy Water and Rich Man'sTerror).

Leader: Hin-in-in

By now Fiery Eye should be off with his mother. Let's wait here to verify.

(Shortly a man appears, carrying a bag).

Leader: Rich Man's Terror, it's time.

> The man that's approaching is a rich man. He has two wives, one of them is pregnant. She'sgoing to be deliver of the baby soon. As soon as he gets here, follow him.

Rich Man's Terror: Thank you very much leader, we shall meet on the appointed day, and in peace.

Rich Man: *(Passes the crossroads. He hears footsteps behind him but does not see or hear anyone).*

> Who is that trailing so closely behind me? What kind of omen is this? (He returns home). There's something fishy.

(At the entrance to his house his wife Àlàkẹ́ meets him).

Àlàkẹ́: Welcome, you've returned early. This is unusual.

> How was business?

Rich Man: I have not been to the shop today.

> I sensed something ominous as I reached Ona Ola junction and I decided to come back home.

Àlàkẹ́: Yeee!

Rich man: What's wrong?

Àlàkẹ́: It's as if something forced its way into my womb.

Rich Man: There shall be no evil,

> so there is no cause for alarm.

(They go inside).

> (As the leader of the familiar spirits and Mammy Water are walking about simultaneously as Rich Man's Terror is entering Àlàkẹ́'s womb, they see a pregnant woman).

Leader: Mammy Water Congratulations.

> That's your mother that's approaching. She is meek, she is a textile dealer and has had no child. Her husband really tried before she got pregnant with the baby she is carrying. Unfeigned love exists between her and her husband.

Mammy Water: That's the type of mother I desire.

Her sorrow shall know no bounds when I die suddenly. What does her husband do for a living?

Leader: He is a trader.

I had all the facts on my finger-tips before connecting her to you.

Mammy Water: That's splendid.

It's time to go. My regards to Little Devil whenever you meeting the air.

(She enters the woman's womb).

Sẹ̀gi: *(Sensing that something has entered her womb)*

What is this? My husband must hear this. I can no longer go on my trip *(she returns home).*

Leader: *(praises himself).*

If no one praises me, I shall praise myself, I have played my leadership role well. I am expecting gnashing of teeth from human beings. I want to see how their mouths will be shaped on the day of sorrow. Rounded or flat?

ACT 2, SCENE 1

(At Olóríẹgbẹ́'s house, people are rejoicing over the birth of a new born baby)

Crowd: *(greeting Ojúufáńtà)*

Congratulations. May God watch over this child? He shall prosper and live long to bear his name. He shall enjoy longevity, and live meaningfully. (Amen)

Old woman: Bring firewood for me.

Let us make fire for the mother and the baby. New babe, new arrival from heaven. He and his mother must not be exposed to cold.

(Pieces of firewood are brought into the room, she arranges some in a tripod).

Get me matches. Olóríẹgbẹ́, give me matches.

Olóríẹgbẹ́: *(goes in and brings matches)* no, no.

Who's the crazy woman that arranged the firewood. Get out, everybody! Out!

Crowd: We have come to rejoice with you.

You don't have to abuse us.

Olóríẹgbẹ́: I'm sorry;

I was just concerned about something. Without a reason woman does not bear Kúmólú. There's a reason behind my action.

(He puts banana trunks inside the tripod instead).

I thank my head, and the hunter as well.

Old woman: Olóríẹgbẹ́, what's the reason behind all your provoked utterances.

Olóríẹgbẹ́: You don't understand, I do.

The child is a mysterious child. A Familiar spirit.

Old woman: How do you know? A new born baby?

Olóríẹgbẹ́: Thank you.

> Ọdẹ́gbàmí alerted me on the matter. He saw familiar spirits at meeting where one of them chose to be our child. He said immediately the first firewood that's put into fire to generate heat for him burns out, he shall return. Since people have learnt wisdom in the intermediary's house, so have people learnt to be wise in the groom's house as well. That's why we arrived at the use of banana trunks instead of firewood.

Ojúufáńtà: I now understand,

> so that's what you and hunter were discussing that day that I went to the farm. My child is not a familiar spirit. How can my first child be a familiar spirit?

(She starts crying)

Olóríẹgbẹ́: (Pleading with her).

> There's no cause for alarm. Don't be afraid. The battle is won. I have dispossessed him of the power of the familiar spirit; joy is ours because a child does not die in the hand of Alákẹdun.

Old woman: Mystery! great mystery!

Crowd: Congratulations. God will make him one of us.

> He will leave to a ripe old age. Olóríẹgbẹ́ is a man.

(*Congratulating him on the safe delivery*).

Olóríẹgbẹ́: (sings, dances)

> Thank you
>
> A child is to be catered for
>
> A child is a garment
>
> A child is a string of wealth
>
> A child is precious

New born babe, visitor to the world

Welcome

I rejoice with you

I cherish a child

It's more desirable than cash

Both the rich and the poor respect children

You people

Dance the dance of the parent with me

New born babe

Ọdẹ́gbàmí thank you.

(He tells a man to go and call Ọdẹ́gbàmí)

Ojo. Go and call Ọdẹ́gbàmí for me. He must be a part of today's celebration. He has made the day.

Olóríẹgbẹ́: *(Exists Ojo, singing and dancing commence).*

(Four hunters accompany Ọdẹ́gbàmí, they entertain the people with Ijálá, the hunter's chant.)

Ọdẹ́gbàmí: (dancing)

I am a hunter

My father is a hunter

A hunter is a hunter

In my father's house

A cause was brought about an elephant that sat

The elders of the town conferred

They couldn't find a way out

They tried

And were at their wit's end

They conferred

And then arrived at a solution

They all gathered

And headed for my father's house

Where they lulled children with *Ide*
There were allegations about the elephant's misdeeds
My father invited elephant's hunter
Saying he was the only one that went with them into the
wild
In the wild
He removed the bow from the sheaths
He took anti-arrow charm
He put a rifle under this hunter's dress
As they approached the spot
Ọdẹ́wálé, can you hear my voice?
The town's inhabitants shouted
That they couldn't enter the elephants
Forest with Ọdẹ́rínú
Its great confusion ensued
A great crisis
Ọdẹ́rínú had the road described to him
And headed for the elephant's forest
After his departure
People began to sorrow over the hunter
Some speculated that an elephant had swallowed him up.
Some said Dérínú had become a python
And swam away
At the end of the day
Dérínú returned unscathed
He proclaimed his conquest of the elephant
They demanded for the elephant's body
Ọdẹ́rìndé cautioned them against cynicism
Saying, the elephant didn't die
It collapsed

Ọdẹrìndé saw elephant had collapsed
He said the elephant was gone
He said if he had known that the elephant
Would fall
Dérínú said he would have held on to the elephant's neck
He would have brought the elephant home
For a forest
He said he would have tried to unravel the mystery
Maybe he would have made history
As the first person to tie the Elephant to the stake
Dérindé
Wilt you chorus the song or not?
Dérindé and others said we shall chorus the song
Other hunter:
The song raised by Aluko is what its child choruses.

Ọdẹgbàmí: *(dancing)*

Ogún, don't let me experience "soso"

Ogun, don't let me experience "soso"

He who invites "soso" will experience "soso".

Hunters: Ogun don't let me experience "soso"

Ọdẹgbàmí: He who invites "soso" will experience "soso"

Hunters: Ogun, don't let me experience "soso"

Ọdẹrìndé: Ogún, you see into the depth of things. If I have offended you. You see deeply into my heart.

Hunters: Ogún sees into the hearts.

Ọdẹrìndé: If I offend you,

You pry into the dark recesses of my mind.

Hunter: Ogún sees deeply into the mind.

Ọdẹ́gbàmí: Satisfied he was.

    Satisfied he was

    The day Ogúndélé ate pounded plantain on the farm.

Hunter: Satisfied he was.

Ọdẹ́gbàmí:

    The day Ogúndélé ate pounded plantain on the farm

Hunters: Satisfied he was.

(They dance off stage)

ACT 2, SCENE 2

(At the Rich Man's house, Àlàkẹ́ rushes out carrying a child).

Àlàkẹ́: Help! He's at it again.

    Bọ́lá is at it again help me! Please help!

Rich Man: What's the matter?

Àlàkẹ́: Bọ́lá has fainted again.

Rich Man: What kind of trouble is this?

    If it's not malaria, it's cold, or head ache.This problem is eating deep into my finances.

Àlàkẹ́: Have you started your lamentation again?

Rich Man: Lord God almighty

    What sin have I committed?

    Those in control of the world

    I ask you

    What trouble is this?

    Why are you fighting against me?

    All the money I ever had

    Bọ́lá has wasted everything

    All the fruit of my sweat

    Has been expended on Bọ́lá's sickness

    All my properties

    Have been wasted on Bọ́lá!

    I am now a pauper

    Total wreck

> I now patch my clothes
> And friends avoid my path
> Efforts to keep the child alive
> Have proved abortive
> All our efforts have turned into child'splay
> I am fed up with life
> And I can't hastily head for heaven
> How can a child be so callous...

Àlàkẹ́: Rich Man, don't be indifferent to my plight.

Please let's do something about this matter. This boy can't just pack up like this.

(With her parents in a state of perplexity, Bọ́lá is at familiar spirit's meeting, laughing at his parent).

Leader: He e eee

He e ee e

He e ee e

My children

Voices: *(Bọ́lá, Rich Man's Terror and Little* Devil)

Yes

Leader: *(Faces Little Devil)*

Little Devil, what's the reason behind this meeting? Any news?

Little Devil: It's a serious matter.

I have conveyed this meeting because of what RichMan's Terror has told me. There is a big problem. It is inconceivable that humans will snatch Fiery Eye from us.

Leader: Impossible! Silence!

Little Devil, stand up, get me my water pot. Let me see what happened that will make human beings try such a thing.

Little Devil: (Hands very a small pot to the leader)

My lord, leader of familiar spirit worldwide, a child cannot die in the hands of the circumciser, a dog cannot kill a cub right behind the tigress. We shall not reduce in number under your leadership.

Leader: *(Stirs the water and starts talking)*

Hooo kakaka rika!

Ka ka ki a rika ooo

Wa yo

Wa yo

You children of men

You cunning people

You have researched

Into snail's liver in the shell

You craftily snatched

Fiery Eye from us

Humans!

Any child that will not allow the mother

To sleep

What shall happen to him?

Let him stay with you

But be assured that you have taken

Your undoing

You have your doomsday!

Little Devil: Leader, who are you talking with?

Leader: Who else can it be? it is Olóríẹgbé and his wife.

Little Devil, draw closer, see them rejoicing! Is it not amazing how people can be weeping but think they are rejoicing?

(Looks and starts talking)

Now, I understand. Henceforth none of you shall ever be missing again. Things must not go awry under my leadership.

A multitudinous sea of humans cannot overcome me. Any powerful individual that again blockades a familiar spirit will have himself to blame. Such an individual courts losses, debts and other afflictions of life. May it be so (spits). As his children are dying so will his wife be stricken by sickness? Unmitigated evils will befall the person. Whoever attempts to wipe out familiar spirits will himself be wiped out.

Little Devil: Leader

Can't we take back Rich Man'sTerror today?

Leader: Shut your trap!

To recall Rich Man's Terror today? You want me to curse you? Who is that medicine man that can withstand me? I shall wipe them out. Let Rich Man's Terror disappear before me straight-way. Insult!

That kind of thing will never happen again. Rich Man's Terror should go. I want to see that mighty man that will snatch him from me.

Little Devil:

Let's increase the power of Rich Man'sTerror to enable him do more exploits in the world.

Leader: That's a good idea.

Call him back

(It's too late. Back In the world, Richman's terror is being woken up at Richman's house).

Rich Man: Àlàké, this is a perplexing case!

This child seems poised to die. Quickly go and bring my rosary and the bottle of miracle water.

(Re-enters Àlàké)

Rich Man: (hangs the rosary on Rich Man's Terror's neck and sprinkles him with water)

In Jesus' name

In Jesus' name

In the mighty name of Jesus

Jehovah father

Manifest the power in this water

Raise Bọlá up

Thou living God

Restore him for me

Reveal yourself as the living God

You that answer prayers

Hear my voice

Bọlá o!

Bọlá o!

Bọlá: Sir…

(Rich Man wipes her face with water)

Àlàkẹ: Thank you God *(sings)*

Thank you Jesus

Thank you Jesus

My daughter that was asleep

Is now awake

Thank you Jesus

My daughter that was asleep

Is now joyfully awake

Thank you Jesus

(Rich Man and Àlàkẹ sing, pull Bọlá off the stage).

ACT 2, SCENE 3

(Rich Man and Àlàké become ardent Christians. The scene takes place in a church).

Congregation: *(Singing and clapping, the pastor is directing affairs)*

    I. *I have not given enough thanks*

       I will give thanks everyday

       I have not given enough thanks

       I shall rejoice everyday.

    II. *I shall give thanks*

       I shall give thanks

       I shall give thanks

       Jesus has done so much for me

       I thank you father.

    III. *There is power*

       There is power

       There is power in the blood of Jesus.

Pastor: *(faces Rich Man)*

Rich Man, the living God has asked me to tell you that Bọlá is your problem. She's the one that is not giving you rest of mind. The Lord says she is a familiar spirit. He says you should bring her before his presence. The Lord says that although she is getting set to return to where she came from. He promises that he shall do a miracle. He will not allow that child to die. Bring her for laying of hands.

Rich Man: *(calls for his driver)*

Sùnmọnù, go and bring Bọlá from home. Make sure you

bring her.

Sùnmọ́nù: The fuel in the car is almost exhausted.

Rich man: No problem, take this money. Bye.

Pastor: Praise the Lord.

Congregation: Hallelluyah.

Pastor: Praise Him.

Congregation: Hallelluyah.

(They sing and dance. Light fades in stage.)

ACT 2, SCENE 4

(Bọ́lá is asleep when Sùnmọ́nù arrives at Rich Man's house. She's attending another meeting of familiar spirits).

Little Devil: Rich Man's Terror

Rich Man's Terror: Little Devil,

> a rodent does not appear in the daylight without a reason. What's the matter? What of the leader?

Little Devil: There's no problem.

> The leader says I should remind you that today is the Dday. We're preparing for you in the air.

Rich Man's Terror: I personally I'm ready.

> The leaf is bound to honour its appointment with the ground. It's part of what I discussed with the leader the other time. What gives you the impression that I don'twant to see you?

Little Devil: Forget about that.

> Meet me in the air straight-away. You must not give those woe-befallen people a chance. The secret of familiar spirits must remain secret. If the secrets are going to become common knowledge, it must not be from you.

Rich Man's Terror: Impossible! Never.

> The secrets will not be blown open by me, or through me. I shall reach you in a short while.

Little Devi: Come right now.

> So that we can plunge the world to shame. (exits)

Rich Man's Terror: *(Soliloquizes)*

> I, Rich Man's Terror, a strong man who can contend with

Eṣu?
Who can contend with Ṣàngó?
Today is the D-day
If we're going on a trip
And we set the date at twenty years
If we're undertaking a journey
And we set the date as thirty months
On the appointed day
The pilgrim must go back home
Today is the appointed day
I shall not go alone
All we Rich Man's children shall go together
When I reach the air
I shall burst into derisive laughter
I shall make jest of the Rich Man
After all Jesus himself said
My kingdom is not of this world
So what am I waiting for?
Mother thinks she is clever
Father thinks he is wise
I, unmatchable familiar spirit
When I get into the air
I shall match confidently like a soldier

Sùnmọ́nù: *(Wakes Bọ́lá)*

Bọ́lá, Bọ́lá

Bọ́lá: Yes.

Sùnmọ́nù: Father says I should bring you to the church
now before the service is over.

Bọ́lá: Is father there?

Sùnmọ́nù: Yes, hurry up, let's go.

Bọlá: It's alright. Let me brush my teeth

(sings)

> This world is not my own
>
> I'm just passing by
>
> All the problems of this life…
>
> Don't let me pass in vain…
>
> Let's go, wait, let's lock all doors so that all other children can go with us

Sùnmọ́nù: That's good.

(all enter the car, on their way to the church, the vehicle is involved in an accident. The noise attracts the attention of worshippers who rush out of the church).

Crowd: Haa! Rich Man's car! All the occupants are dead.

Man: Let's rush them to the hospital.

(notices that Bọlá is still breathing)

> This one is still alive. She sustained just minor injuries.

Congregation: *(They carry Bọláto the church, while the dead are conveyed to the hospital).*

> This is terrible. The driver and other occupants of the car are dead.
>
> *(The Rich Man faints, the service is thrown into pandemonium)*

Pastor: Please pour miracle water on him

(they resuscitate the Rich Man, and bath for Bola)

> Rich Man, don't be sad. Let Bọlá come forward for prayer *(they kneel in front of pastor)*
>
> In Jesus' name
>
> In Jesus' name
>
> In the mighty name of Jesus
>
> Jehovah father
>
> Solely in the authority of the name of Jesus

I bring this boy before you

By the mighty power in the name of Jesus

I command

Because fire burns on the basis of divine authority

The sun shines on the basis of its divine mandate

Bọlá, confess, what type of child are you?

Thou living God,

Expose the secret of familiar spirits- Amen

Confess. Amen

Jesus, take control of his heart. Amen.

That he may confess. Amen.

In the name of Jesus. Amen.

Amen. Amen.

Amen. Amen.

Amen. Amen.

Bọlá: *(burst into tears as they open their eyes, tries to tear off her rosary from her neck)*

This useless rosary is the cause.

Pastor: In the name of Jesus, the Prince of Peace,

I command you to confess the type of child you are before the people of God.

Bọlá: My real name is Rich Man's Terror.

I am a familiar spirit. This is the very day I'm billed to go back. I have been hindering my father's progress. Also, I blocked my mother from having more children. I caused the death of my siblings because it had been ordained that they should all die with me.

Pastor: *(Rings his bell)*

Halleluyah

Is that all?

Bọlá: Yes

Pastor: Where do you normally hold your meetings?

Bọlá: In the air, at night.

> When we are going for meetings, we will face the wall while sleeping, our right feet uplifted. Nobody would attempt to wake us in that posture, till we return. Sand and unripe banana is our food. We drink greenwater.

Pastor: How many people have you killed?

Bọlá: Apart from the incident of today, I've never killed anyone.

Pastor: Are you going back to your group?

Bọlá: Now that I have confessed my sins in the presence of the Lord, Jesus has taken control of my heart. I no longer belong to the familiar spirit society.

Pastor: Shout Halleluyah!

Congregation: Halleluyah!

Pastor: Are there further suffering you want to inflict on your parents?

Bọlá: No

Pastor: *(Faces the congregation)*

> People of God, learn a great lesson from this. Those of you who claim there's no familiar spirit, have you seen ?
>
> Let us pray
>
> In Jesus name, let the life of this child be transformed today.
>
> That he will know the way of God,
>
> Let it be so. Amen.

(Faces Rich Man)

> Fear not, the battle is over. Jesus has healed you. The warning is that everybody should fast on Friday and we should all assemble here at six o'clock on that day for a special prayer. Jesus will answer our prayer. Amen

Go ahead with your song:
Jesus spread gift all over
I pack mine
Jesus spread gift all over
I pick mine

(Light fades)

ACT 3, SCENE1

(*At the house of Túndùn (Fúnmi or Mammy Water's mother), Àlàdé (Funmi's father) is crying*).

Túndùn: (*Wakes Àlàdé fearfully*).

Bàbá Fúnmi! Bàbá Fúnmi!! Fúnmi has not returned home since she left in the morning and it's about three o' clock now. What shall we do?

Àlàdé: Where did you send her to?

Is Fúnmi a baby? Just tell me where you sent her.

Túndùn: You handle everything with levity!

She told me she was going to her friend's house to read. It appears there's more to this girl's issue than meet the eye.

Àlàdé: You are entitled to your opinion.

Fúnmi is not a kid.

Túndùn: Babá Fúnmi!

This girl's issue deserves serious attention. Where shall I run to? This girl is acting as if she belongs to the spirit World.

Àlàdé: What are the proofs?

People will take a cue from you on whatever you call your child. If you like give your daughter a tag. People will take a cue from you.

Túndùn: Are Fúnmi's behaviours not questionable?

It's alright. Last week, Fúnmi did wonders! She came to my shop. You know sales have been dull for some time. She came with a preparation which she dissolved in water and used to smear the four corners of the shop. That day, buyers besieged the shop.The trend has continued till today.

Àlàdé: Where did she bring the preparation?

Túndùn: It's a surprise to me.

I wanted to flog her that day, but she ran away. She claimed itwas given to her by a friend. She even took a roll of Àṅkárá to her invisible friend. Till now, she is yet to tell me reason behind her action.

Àlàdé: Túndùn! Túndün!! Are you out of your mind?

If those who buy on credit from you have not received their salary, can they pay you?

Túndùn: All right.

Can't you recall what happened the day I was complaining about money here?

Àlàdé: The day you were going to buy goods?

Túndùn: *(claps)*

BàbáFúnmi, your daughter pulled me to a corner. She directed me to the corner of the house where she said I would find money. I thought it was a joke. I saw fifty thousand naira there. She mandated me to spend the money.

Àlàdé: *(laughs).* Exaggerations!

You're blowing everything beyond proportion. If she possesses such powers, Why then are we toiling? God has blessed us!

Túndùn: BàbáFúnmi, this is a serious matter

Or do you think it is something you can trivialize?

Àlàdé: If all these things are true,

why haven't you told me all this while?

Túndùn: All these happenings were like child's play

compared to what happened yesterday.

Àlàdé: What did she do?

Túndùn: Her mates came here yesterday evening to say

that her teacher would like to see me.

Àlàdé: What happened?

Túndùn: There was a problem.

The teacher reported that some of the pupils said they would like to eat pounded yam with goat meat where they were playing. Fúnmi said she would give it to them if they would keep the secret. Her mates testified that my daughter conjured pounded yam and goat meat for them. The teacher showed me the food as evidence.

Àlàdé: Are you sure?

Túndùn: The teacher and Fúnmi's mates will confirm the story if you ask them.

Àlàdé: The situation is getting out of hand.

Yet I don't want to subscribe to the idea that Fúnmi is a familiar spirit according to the medicine man. Something has to be done about it.

Túndùn: It's a matter that can no longer be swept under the carpet. No matter how hard we try to pretend about it, it's a keg of gunpowder that we are sitting upon. What shall we do? Her illness has in addition become a conduit pipe that's draining us of money. Unfortunately, she's our only child. She shouldn't be allowed to drown.

Àlàdé: *(Pleads with her)*

Don't take it so hard. Stop crying. It's a joint task. We were only lax. Once our enemy has been exposed, the battle is halfwon. Arise, I am heading for Awógbèmí's house.

(Túndùn goes inside)

There shall be no delay. Off I go to Awógbèmí's house.

(Light fades).

ACT 3, SCENE 2

(In a bush, a meeting of familiar spirit is in progress. Leader, Little Devil and Mammy Water are in attendance).

Leader: (Sweating profusely)

Little Devil: The earth is depleted

The world is ruined

They want to turn familiar spirits into a plaything

They have invited trouble

They shall see trouble

There shall be no pardon

It's everlasting sorrow

They shall experience unending gnashing of teeth

They have held Fiery Eye to ransom

They have also seized Rich Man's Terror

They must pay for it

There is no forgiveness

The children of men must suffer

Mammy Water

What further measures can we take?

Shake off this shame?

Familiar spirit shall not go into

Extinction under my leadership!

Familiar spirit shall not die

Never! Not under my leadership!

Not under yours too either

The human race will pay dearly

From their intransigence

As their intransigence

As they wail

And gnash their teeth

You shall be glad

And rejoice

Because familiar spirits assembly cannot scattered.

Little Devil and Mammy Water:

Your majesty, do we have any mountain that is higher than you?

You're our father

The father that is greater

Than every other father

Your majesty.

Leader: Little Devil, what's the matter?

Little Devil: I have convened this meeting in an effort to

deliver Mammy Water from the hands of mankind. The wisdom of human beings is worrisome. It's really disturbing. I'm scared.

Leader: Mammy Water,

what do you have to say on this issue?

Mammy Water: Thank you.

Little Devil has been forthright in his statement. It seems as if those miserable people are suspicious of me but who is that policeman that can arrest the wind? All their efforts on me will end in futility.

Leader: Mammy Water.

Mammy Water: I am serious.

What is that thing that can entangle the elephant? Mine is completely different from those that have been arm twisted, I may be compassionate but whoever attempts to separate me from my fellow familiar spirits will pay dearly for it. Whoever tries to arrest me will have himself or herself to blame. Who can arrest the wind? Who is that person that can trace the source of the sea? I am a dry bone, human beings cannot arrest me.

Leader: I have nothing to fear as far as you are concerned.

Let me do head washing for you (he washes Mammy Water's head with green water). Mammy Water, you may go. It's in vain that the leg desires to crack the palm nut along the wayside. Go.

Together: (*They sing somberly*)

We quintessential familiar spirits

That put medicine men to shame

Invisible children that contend with the cultists that wreck the affluent

We reduce the able-bodied to handicapped souls

Before we deal the final blow

We send cold shivers

Down the spine of humans

Terror of the air that invades the town

Imperious deaths that kill in cold blood

Go back to the world

With added power

And added knowledge

Go back to the world

(*They disperse*)

(*Light fades on stage*)

ACTS 3, SCENE 3

(Alade's house)

Túndùn: *(meets Fúnmi as she comes out of the house)*

> Fúnmi, where have you been? You are a accursed child, naughty,useless, irresponsible wretch, a mere effigy! I will teach you a lesson today *(crying)*

Fúnmi: If you beat me, you will regret your action.

Túndùn: *(Slaps Fúnmi)*

Fúnmi: You raise your hand to slap me.

> Nobody ever raises his or her hand to slap my face. Abomination! What you've done is a taboo. You have gone beyond your bounds. (Fúnmi transforms into an old woman). Who told you that my name is Fúnmiláyọ̀? I pronounce anguish upon you from today. I, Mammy Water. You shall remain barren for the rest of your life. You shall die barren. Túndun, you have reached the crossroads, and you shall never know the way out. You are in for it (she starts laughing, falls into a swoon).

Túndùn: *(with trepidation)*

> Help! Help! Come to my aid.
>
> People from the neighbourhood
>
> I am in trouble.

Crowd: Fúnmi! Fúnmi! Fúnmi! Oh!

> But we saw this girl a short while ago.
>
> She even greeted us

(They try to resuscitate Fúnmi)

Man: Where is her father?

Tundùn: Help me, he has gone out!

Àlàdé: (Enters with Awógbàmí)

What's the problem?

Crowd: It's Fúnmi

Àlàdé: Awógbàmí. I'm finished.

> This is an irreplaceable loss, sorrow in the twilight of life.
> Awógbàmí, come to my aid. Don't let me be put to shame.

Awógbàmí: *(Brings out a bag from under his dress)*

> Don't be terrified. Ọ̀rúnmìlà will give mean insight. Aje
> leaf cannot fail.
>
> Sweet water flows from my mother's eye
>
> We cannot mention Emèrè without pronouncing its last
> syllable
>
> I know you all
>
> Familiar spirits of the world
>
> You use yellow water to dispossess people of their chil-
> dren
>
> We use orange colour water to rescue them
>
> If Fúnmi is one of you
>
> Release her with dispatch
>
> Because when fire burns child
>
> The child removes his hand quickly
>
> When yèrèpe hurts a child
>
> The child quickly calls his mother
>
> This is fire
>
> It has burnt your hands
>
> Release Fúnmi
>
> Excreta does not attract he who passed it
>
> Fúnmi has become
>
> The foul smell of excreta

Release her

Fúnmi!

My mother says you are Mammy Water

A child must response to the sound of its name

We know it thrice

We call it thrice

Funmi ò!

Fúnmi ò!

Fúnmi o!

Mammy Water o!

Mammy Water o!

Mammy Water

Fúnmi: Yes! *(opens her eyes)*

Leader, don't leave me. Take me along with you, I, princess of familiar spirits.

Leader, deliver me, don't put me to shame among human beings.

(As she is speaking Awógbàmí is wiping her face with lime water).

Awógbàmí: *(hits Fúnmi on the chest thrice)*

Fúnmi, this is a decree. It is enough.

Because Ṣàngó kills a tree for both good and evil.

Any tree that Ṣàngó kills does not contend with Ṣàngó

Emo order you to keep shut

A machete does not fight while still In its sheathe

We do not gather to speak despitefully of a lover

Enough is enough. Come back to the world to be a child.

(puts seven alligator pepper in his mouth)

Whatever we tell ọgbọ́ is what ọgbọ́ hears

Whatever we tell ọgbà is what ọgbà hears

Ọgbọ́ cannot be too big to disobey the deity

The earth must accede to the rodent's wish

Any animal attacked by the cobra

Dies in cobra's mouth

Black thread

White thread

Cannot argue with each other

Whatever I command must be obeyed

Fúnmi, return to the world

Come and comfort your parents

From today, get out of the camp of familiar spirits

(Fúnmi becomes composed)

Awógbàmí: Àlàdé, you and Túndùn should see me at
home when Fúnmi finishes eating. Don't let anybody stay
with her (exits Awógbàmí).

Crowd: Such an evil shall never re-occur in your home.

God will grant her long life.

(They disperse)

ACT 3, SCENE 4

(Awógbàmí's house - a typical herbalist setting).

Awógbàmí: Kékeré, bring the ọ̀pẹ̀lẹ̀ and ìrọ́kẹ̀.

Today is a great day.

(He sings ìyẹ̀rẹ̀ song. Kékeré the apprentice medicine man choruses it, and Awógbàmí bangs his ọ̀pẹ̀lẹ̀ on the ground)

Ifá will always speak the truth - Hin-In

Ifá has never spoken falsehood - Hin-in

Ifá will always speak whatever he sees - Hin-In

Ọ̀pẹ̀lẹ̀ will tell the world only what it sees Hin

Cause Ifa to be involved in the issue of a familiar spirit- Hin-in

They consulted Ifa on her behalf - Hin-in

Ifa said everything will be all right - Hin-in

Ifa said they should offer a sacrifice - Hin-in

They said what type of sacrifice Hin-in

Ifa said familiar spirit's load should be packed -Hin-in

He said they should buy white calabash - Hin-in

He said white cloth is inclusive - Hin-in

Palm-oil is part of the ingredients - Hin-in

He said they should buy a big animal - Hin-in

He added they should provide one hundred and forty cow-ries - Hin-In

Plenty of beans - Hin-in

Bitter kola and kolanut also - Hin-in

They should look for heavy plantain trunk -Hin-in

They should make a coffin that's worth two thousand- Hin-in

They did everything - Hin-in

The sacrifice was accepted - Hin-in

The familiar spirit stayed Hin-in

She became wealthy and had children -Hin-in

It is courtesy of Ifa- Hin-in

The then acclaimed familiar spirit stayed - Hin-in

She became wealthy and bore children - Hin-in

Ọrúnmilà the wise one

Guardian of the orphan - Hin-In

The wise one Awógbàmí's father - Hin-in

We shall continue to enjoy your largesse

We shall continue to enjoy your largesse

Don't allow your own life to suffer in the world

We shall continue to enjoy your largesse.

(Àlàdé and Túndùn knock at the door)

Awógbàmí: Are you initiated or uninitiated?

Àlàdé: Uninitiated

Awógbàmí: Enter

Àlàdé and Túndun: Your sacrifice will continue to be accepted.

Awógbàmí: Ọrúnmilà will aid you

Aladé and Túndùn: Thank you,

Ọrúnmilà will not expose you to shame. The almighty will stand by you.

Awógbàmí: Let's praise Ifá. Ifá is worthy of praise,

it's not by my power. Its Ọrúnmilà's doing. There's still work to be done. Infact you met me on it. She's a chieftain in the familiar spirits realm. She's Mammy Water. She's also a matron. Are you ready for the remaining task?

Àlàdé: What shall we do?

Awógbàmí: It is simple. Ifa has seen it all.

> We shall pack the familiar spirits load for her. It's a bit costly.

Túndùn: How much? We're ready to pay.

> On this child I am prepared to do anything to preserve her life.

Àlàdé: Tundùn, take it easy.

> Are you the one that will spend the money?

Awógbàmí: Plenty words cannot fill a basket.

> If a male sees a snake and a female kills it, the important thing is that the snake is killed. This child shall not die. She has nowhere to go. Her palms will cover us.

Àlàdé: How much is the money?

Awógbàmí: I won't take money from you.

> Listen carefully for the items you will purchase. A white calabash to pack the items, white cloth, a female goat, one hundred and forty cowries, beans, a coffin, nine bitter kola and a banana trunk. Bring those items along with Fúnmi.

Túndùn: Bàbá, Fúnmi will not come

Awógbàmí: Mention my name to her.

> She will follow you like a hunter's dog.

(Àlàdé goes to buy the items)

***

Túndùn: Bàbá, Fúnmi's father lingers.

Awógbàmí: Be patient. He'll soon be here.

(Àlàdé enters in company of Fúnmi)

> Àlàdé, welcome Fúnmi, daughter of deity, we're friends, and can't afford to fight. I am doing everything in the interest of your parents, so they don't die childless, I beg you, let our sacrifice be accepted. Let them die peacefully.

Fúnmi: There is no problem.

Let's join hands to make all well for them. But make it clear to them that I am an unusual child. Due to your involvement, I shall not die anymore and I promise to take care of them. Not only, that, even after their departure from the world I shall do them proud.

Awógbàmí: The sacrifice has been accepted.

Àlàdé, pack that banana trunk like a corpse.

Put it on the coffin and put all the other items but the calabash inside. Kékeréawo, wrap the white cloth around Fúnmi and paint her with chalk.

Àlàdé and Awógbàmí: It's time for action.

A leaf cannot fail in its appointment with the earth. Kékeré, place the calabash on Fúnmi's head, let Àlàdé carry the coffin. Túndùn shall follow us quietly. What are we waiting for? Let's go.

(They exit).

ACT 3, SCENE 55

(In thick bush where there's a flowing river. Fúnmi goes in front, followed by Kékeréawo, Túndùn, Àlàdé and Awógbami wrap white cloth around their loins. Àlàdé and Túndùn are dressed in white bùbá and white trousers. Awógbàmí and Kékeréawo beat a gong as they go along)

All: We are heading for the river of the world,

> A river that people consider as ordinary water that the ignorant just drink an important river that's the seat of the world's Familiar spirits.

> The hideout of spirit children is in trouble

> We're going to the river

> We're heading for the river

> We're definitely going to the river

> We're going to the river

> We're going to the river

> We're surely going to the river

> We're going to the river of the world

> Which the ignoramuses drink

> An important river that's the seat of

> The world familiar spirits

> The hideout of spirit children is in trouble

> We're going to the river

> We're going to the river

> We're going to the river

> We're going to the river

We're definitely going to the river

River of familiar spirits

Mysterious river

We're going to the river

(Close to the river bank)

Awógbàmí: Stop! Stop!

(They stand)

We've reached the river bank. Àlàdé, it's time for your action. Put down the coffin. Túndùn and Kékeréawo, stand by the coffin Fúnmi, move to the front with your calabash.

Alàdé, follow her, I am coming behind.

(They sing)

An out of the way place

River of trouble

We've come with sacrifice

Death should flee

Sickness should flee

Death should go beneath the earth

Sickness should disappear

Familiar spirit should be peaceful

The world should now rest

The city should be peaceful

River of trouble

River of trouble

Hear our voice

Let our sacrifice be accepted

The power of familiar spirits should perish

Mother should give birth

Her children should live

Mother and her children should play happily together

The world should be peaceful

The world should go about its business peacefully.

(At the river bank)

Awógbàmí: Funmi, put down your calabash.

(Awógbàmí lifts the calabash from the ground and starts chanting incantations)

Familiar spirit river

I have reached the place of crowning leaf

Familiar spirit I've come

Today is the D-day

We've come with Fúnmi's group load

Calabash floats *tente* on the water

These items are yours today

Accept the load

Let evil go with it

Let it go with premature death

Let it attract wealth

It should bring longevity, which is even better than wealth

Fúnmi should quit familiar spirit realms, be merciful to Àlàdé that he will have more children.

It's our desire that children will survive us, familiar spirit, accept this sacrifice.

This package is for the group

Kindly accept us in our low estate

If we sew a garment for a lazy man

We also dye it for him

Familiar spirit river

Pull us out completely

Whoever you deliver receives total deliverance

Don't make this a partial gift

Deliver us totally

Awógbàmí: Fúnmi, cast the calabash into the river.

If it floats, sacrifice is accepted. If it doesn't, we have to start over again.

(Fúnmi throws the calabash into the river, it floats. Awógbàmí instructs Fúnmi to say after him)

It is the departure of dragon-fly that we see

Nobody ever sees its return

The package for the group

You are going

We shall never meet again

Familiar spirits death should spare me

Power of familiar spirit should have no influence on me

Because a child has no power over osè tree

The sun must run its normal course

Alligator pepper always has its children intact

Familiar spirit death should by-pass me

I should become an important personality

I should be useful to my father

I should become a real child to my mother

I should become useful in the family

I should become a channel of blessing to my friends from today

I cease to be a child of sorrow

I should become a beloved child

I should become an enviable personality

I should be honoured at home

I should be honoured abroad

My peers should love me

Familiar spirits should reject me

A small white calabash
Immaculate white cloth
I am sparkling white, and can no longer suck blood
I choose to live from today
I am transformed
Into a new babe
I am oyílàkí
A possessor of multi-dimensional beauty
I am *ajíginni*
I am *arìnginni*
I walk *gìnnìgìnnì* into market
No one can out of anger hit *ipín* with an axe
Familiar spirits reject me
Don't attack me
No one ties *orimogajia's* child with rope
Familiar spirit untie me unfailingly
Good evening is *agbena's* voice
Make way is *arikun's* cry
Little children
That enter the forest without bowing down
to Ago
Get stung by bees
(Greets Ago with whistling)
Ago
I greet "Ago"
Familiar spirit
Make way for me
Let me be celebrated
Let me become an infant
That I shall enjoy on earth

That I shall make headway

Because Ṣàngó kills trees for good and evil at ire

Any tree killed by Ṣàngó

Cannot query Ṣàngó

Emo has ordered you to keep quiet

No machete can fight while in its sheathe

People do not gather to mock a lover

Familiar spirit

From today

We are enemies

Emo has ordered you my enemies to steer clear of me

I have become a beloved child

Familiar spirits should hold no parley on me

Familiar spirits of the world

Familiar spirit on the heavenlies

I part ways with you

A river does not flow backwards

Bye

(Awógbàmí beats the gong thrice)

Awógbàmí: Fúnmi, arise, you and your father.

Go and meet Kékeréawo and Tundun up stream, I am com-ing *(stays back)*

Familiar spirit river

Whatever we tell *Ogbá*

Ogbà accepts

Ogbo cannot be so big

To ignore *Orisa's* voice

Whatever the rodent tells the earth

Is what the earth hears

Any animal attacked by the cobra is done for

Fire leaf hurts quickly
A child plucks *esisi* leaf quickly
Salt obey the palm oil
Wherever oil is poured
Is a path for ants
A fly needs not recognize us
Before perching on us
Whatever we do today
Should be drawn by òǹfa
Should become a changeless decree
All men are wizards
Be involved in it
You that kill without sharing the bones
Midnight celebrities
Deliver me
Owners of the world
Deliver me
Stamp it
That this won't be my end
It won't be my last assignment
So be it, so be it, so be it *(spits)*

(He joins others)

Awógbàmí: Àlàdé, Kékeré, dig the ground.

We have coffin today.

Àlàdé: *(after some time).* We are through.

Awógbàmí: Túndùn, hold Fúnmi's left hand and touch the hand thrice with your mouth. Alàdé, you and Kékeréawo should bury the coffin.

(As they do, Awógbàmí continues)

Mammy Water we bury you today.

Forever, familiar spirit should not visit our home
Fúnmi, we bury your familiar spirit
We separate you forever
You shall live long
And prosper
And shall prosper
You shall prosper
You shall be rich
You shall make it
Familiar spirit shall never visit you again
Because the instant a goat looks back
It returns a curse to the owner
The moment a sheep looks back
It returns a curse to the one who uttered it
If a person gives a sheep to a masquerade
He releases the rope
Familiar spirits reject you
They reject you in the world
They reject you in heaven. So be it.
(He bursts into singing, drumming and gong beating go along)
Congratulations Àlàdé
Fire outbreak does not kill àwòdi
Congratulations àwòdi
Congratulation Túndùn
Fire outbreak does not kill àwòdì
Congratulations àwòdì
Congratulations Fúnmiláyọ̀
Fire outbreak does not kill àwòdì
Congratulations àwòdì
(They dance off stage)

(By a wall in a corner, familiar spirits leader and Little Devil are seated, downcast. They are dressed in robes made of cowries)

Leader: (*furious*)

   Little Devil, be comforted. It's all right. Hun-in

   The world does not know yet

   That familiar spirits are not to be toyed with

   The world has committed a sacrilege

   They snatched my child

   And they think they can go scot free

   The familiar spirits I will send to the world now

   Will be like *wèrèpè*

   No one will be able to tame them

   They will afflict humans on every side unceasingly

   What power can tame them?

   Wizards and witches?

   You're too small!

   Loss of children

   Loss of money

   Loss of health

   All will befall human beings

   Medicine men you are in trouble

   Herbalist will hit a brick wall

   Pastor where are you?

   Hunters, death will be your portion

   Herbalist, shame on you

   All of you are in trouble

   You better exile yourself into villages

   And leave the town for us

   Over-ripe pregnancy will be rampant

   Financial losses will overflow

As people complain of money
They will lament over barrenness
Those that manage to give birth
Shall be plunged into sorrow on marriage ceremony days
They shall fall down dead on their days of happiness
In the season of lifting
They will splash pepper on mother's face
They will lie helpless like wood logs
A leaf must keep faith its appointment with the earth
Familiar spirits are no playthings
It is rain that beat the broken wall
That makes the goat climb it
It is rain that beats the pigeon
That makes it to be dumped with hens
Don't you know us?
People should not meet us
But the world has met us
They say people must not kill vulture
But you inhabitants of the world
Have killed the vulture
And even eaten the meat!
The matter is a crisis for the world
You have courted trouble
Now abide in anguish
You will be shivering
There shall be no ease
Left, right and centre
We rejuvenated
We've gone back to the drawing board
We shall not be afflicted

A second time

Little Devil, give me the little black gourd.

We're back from drawing board

Little Devil: Here, it is.

Of what use is this in the face of the massive onslaught against us?

Leader: A child labels a charm a vegetable out of sheer

ignorance. You will see. If a child has many attire as an adult, can he have as many rags. Raises it up as high as possible (goes round Little Devil seven times) if this bottle drops from your hand, it means that your war with humans is going to be victorious. If it doesn't fall, it means we are going to over-run the human race with ease.

(He brings out a black handkerchief, and wipes his face)

The seven powers of the world

The seven powers of the dark forest

The seven powers of the sea that's the king waters!

The seven powers of the Ocean that destroys the net!

The seven powers of *Èṣù* at the crossroads

Terrific speed is the house rat's

Come from the north

Come from the east

Let the earth tremble

Shake the leaves heavily

Wear robes of fire

Come and burn humans

Come quickly

To adjudge

Whether it is humans that are powerful

Or we familiar spirit

Reveal

If air is blown into a child's eye

He will see

Are we going to be victorious in this battle?

Or are we going to be defeated?

The spirits that live in the wild

Reveal

Reveal

Reveal

(The small calabash drops from the Little Devil's hand. It breaks, and the black water inside spills all round).

Leader: Humans

Children of Adam

Has an end come to familiar spirits?

(He holds the Little Devil's hand, and they mumble as they go off stage).

Whether it is the land squirrel

That owns the farm

Or the trap

It's time to know

We shall meet again

We shall squeeze bitter leaf liquid into human eyes

Humans will know that they have on their head, the bee tree

Thorns will enter their eyes

They will beg us

We shall ignore their plea

Little Devil

We are now hunters

Let's get set to pounce

Let's look for vulnerable games

People should carry their corpse
Let the people of the city hear
And convey the message to those in village
Let the herbalist hear
And inform the pastor
Hunters should beware
Because we have reached the crossroads
Whether in sitting
Or standing posture
The world has hung one leg, and is standing on one.
So that familiar spirit will not to go into extinction
It is imperative that we break the lone foot
Upon which the world limps
And render it a paralytic.
Humans
Children of Adam
Where is your refuge?
That familiar spirit will not humiliate you?
That there will be no vengeance?
That you will gnash your teeth?
That familiar spirit will not rejoice with you?
That we shall not expose you to ridicule?
Because a goat cannot open up its mouth to eat salt without finishing its earthly journey
Humans
Children of Adam
How do you plan
To wriggle out of the torments
By familiar spirits of the world?
(They mumble out of the stage)

THE END.

QUESTIONS

Act 1

1. In one word describe the appearance of the Leader of the Familiar Spirits. Describe his role.

2. Who brought Fiery Eye to the group?

3. Who was in charge of their financial record?

4. Who was rude to the Leader?

5. Narrate the request of the following members of the Familiar Spirits:

    (i) Fiery Eye

    (ii) Rich Man's Terror

    (iii) Mammy Water

6. Explain the operations of each of the above-mentioned name.

7. What transpired between the Hunter and Olóríẹgbẹ́?

8. What happened to Àlàkẹ́ when she shouted "Yeee!"?

Act 2

1. Describe what happened at Olóríẹgbẹ́'s house when his wife, Ojúufáńtà gave birth to a baby.

2. Why did Olóríẹgbẹ́ send for Ọdẹ́gbàmí?

3. What happened at the Rich Man's house when Àlàkẹ́ was crying?

4. Where was Bọ́lá (Familiar Spirit) their daughter when Àlàkẹ́ was crying?

5. How was Bọ́lá revived?

6. Narrate how Bọ́lá was removed from the Familiar Spirit group and the events that led to her removal.

Act 3

1. Mention some instances when Fúnmi's parents began to suspect her as a member of Familiar Spiritmember.

2. What was Fúnmi's reaction when her mother, Túndùn slapped her?

3. Who did Fúnmi's parents run to when he fainted.

4. Describe the process of the sacrifice done by Awógbèmí to preserve Fúnmi's life.

5. Describe what happened in the world of the Familiar Spirits, during the process of the sacrifice.

6. According to this play, mention the ways you think the power of the Familiar Spirits can be conquered.

7. Give this book a befitting title of your choice.

ABOUT THE AUTHOR

Reverend Olatinwo Adeagbo Fatoki

Reverend Ọlátìńwọ́ Adéagbo Fátókí hails from Kúṣeélá, Igbó-Elérin in Lagelu Local Government, Oyo State. He was born on 10th September, 1951.

He attended IDC Primary School, Ode-Aje and Lagelu Grammar School, Agugu, Ibadan for his primary and secondary schools respectively. He then proceeded to Cooperative College, Eleyele, Ibadan. He bagged B.A. Yoruba and Philosophy at the University of Lagos in 1998. He also studied Public Administration at the University of Ife now Obafemi Awolowo University, lle-Ife. He had a Post Graduate Diploma in Public Relations at the Nigerian Institute of Journalism, Ibadan Campus. He also graduated as a Reverend at Immanuel College of Theology in 1991which qualified him to be the Priest of an Anglican Church.

He was a Permanent Secretary at Oyo State Secretariat, Ibadan before he retired in 2007. Among his works are Emèrè (and Familiar Spirit – the English version), Igi Ìṣòkan, Àjẹ́, Àṣàkẹ́ Ọlọ́kọ Mẹ́ta, Àrẹ̀mú Alágbẹ̀dẹ Òrò and Ewì Ìtanijí.
He co-founded Regina James Academy with his late wife Adetola from which union they were blessed with children and grandchildren.